gr. 1

E
MAY
LIT

Mayer, Mercer

Little Critter's
this is my school.

AG 10 '98

LittLE CRitter's
THIS IS MY SCHOOL

BY
MERCER MAYER

For Gina

CULVER-UNION TWP. PUBLIC LIBRARY
107-111 N. MAIN ST.
CULVER-INDIANA 46511
219-842-2941

gr. 1

A Golden Book • New York
Western Publishing Company, Inc., Racine, Wisconsin 53404

© 1990 Mercer Mayer. Little Critter® is a registered trademark of Mercer Mayer. All rights reserved. Printed in the U.S.A. No part of this book may be reproduced or copied in any form without written permission from the publisher. All other trademarks are the property of Western Publishing Company, Inc. Library of Congress Catalog Card Number: 89-82018 ISBN: 0-307-11589-5/ISBN: 0-307-66589-5 (lib. bdg.) A B C D E F G H I J K L M

Today is my first day
of school.

I have new things
to wear.

3

I have a new pencil
and a notebook.

Mom gives me
money for lunch.

Mom gives me
an apple for
the teacher.

But I want
to give the teacher
my new bug.
Mom says an apple
is better.

Mom waits with me
for the school bus.

She does not have to wait,
because I am big.
But it makes her happy.

9

The bus is full.
The driver is quiet.
But we are not.
We are having fun.

I know where to go.
But I ask someone anyway.

My teacher is Miss Kitty.
I give her my apple.

We put our things away.
We have a lot of things!

15

Miss Kitty gives us
name tags.

I sit at my desk.
There are many kids
I do not know.

17

Everyone has to tell
something about himself.
I tell about going camping.
The bear took our food.

We learn a song.
Some kids do not sing.

We draw pictures.
I draw my family.

Then we go play outside.

After playtime Miss Kitty
reads a story.

The bell rings.
It is time for lunch.
I buy lunch
all by myself.

I sit with some
other kids.
We trade food.

24

After lunch we have
rest time.
I am not tired.
But I have to
lie down anyway.

After rest time
we go to the library.

We have the most books
in the world.

We meet the school nurse.

Then we see a film
about dinosaurs.
I am not scared.
Dinosaurs are all
dead anyway.

Then it is time
to go home.

Miss Kitty helps us
onto the bus.

Tomorrow is show-and-tell.
I think I will bring
my pet snake.